P9-APO-021

# Dear Parent:

Congratulations! Your child is taking the first steps on an exciting journey. The destination? Independent reading!

**STEP INTO READING®** will help your child get there. The program offers five steps to reading success. Each step includes fun stories and colorful art. There are also Step into Reading Sticker Books, Step into Reading Math Readers, Step into Reading Phonics Readers, Step into Reading Write-In Readers, and Step into Reading Phonics Boxed Sets—a complete literacy program with something for every child.

## Learning to Read, Step by Step!

### Ready to Read   Preschool–Kindergarten
• big type and easy words • rhyme and rhythm • picture clues
For children who know the alphabet and are eager to begin reading.

### Reading with Help   Preschool–Grade 1
• basic vocabulary • short sentences • simple stories
For children who recognize familiar words and sound out new words with help.

### Reading on Your Own   Grades 1–3
• engaging characters • easy-to-follow plots • popular topics
For children who are ready to read on their own.

### Reading Paragraphs   Grades 2–3
• challenging vocabulary • short paragraphs • exciting stories
For newly independent readers who read simple sentences with confidence.

### Ready for Chapters   Grades 2–4
• chapters • longer paragraphs • full-color art
For children who want to take the plunge into chapter books but still like colorful pictures.

**STEP INTO READING®** is designed to give every child a successful reading experience. The grade levels are only guides. Children can progress through the steps at their own speed, developing confidence in their reading, no matter what their grade.

Remember, a lifetime love of reading starts with a single step!

© 2014 Viacom International Inc. All rights reserved. Published in the United States by Random House Children's Books, a division of Random House, Inc., 1745 Broadway, New York, NY 10019, and in Canada by Random House of Canada Limited, Toronto. Nickelodeon, Team Umizoomi, and all related titles, logos, and characters are trademarks of Viacom International Inc.

Step into Reading, Random House, and the Random House colophon are registered trademarks of Random House, Inc.

Visit us on the Web!
StepIntoReading.com
randomhouse.com/kids

Educators and librarians, for a variety of teaching tools, visit us at RHTeachersLibrarians.com

ISBN 978-0-385-37494-1 (trade) — ISBN 978-0-385-37495-8 (lib. bdg.)

Printed in the United States of America

10 9 8 7 6 5 4 3 2 1

Random House Children's Books supports the First Amendment and celebrates the right to read.

# STEP INTO READING®

nickelodeon TEAM UMIZOOMI™

# TOP COPS

Based on the teleplay by Clark Stubbs

Illustrated by Jason Fruchter

Random House 🏠 New York

Milli, Geo, and Bot are
UmiCops!
They have blue hats
and shiny badges.

# UmiCar has a siren.

"Now we need
a case to solve,"
says Geo.

The Umi Alarm rings!
"Twelve stinkbugs are
making the city stinky,"
says Bot.

"The stinkbugs are hiding in a toy store, a clock shop, and a post office," says Bot.

"It's time for action!"
shouts Team Umizoomi.
UmiCar races
to the toy store.

Four stinkbugs are hiding
behind the toys.
Milli uses Pattern Power
to find them.

The toy pattern should be airplane, sailboat, airplane, sailboat.

"The rocket
should not be there,"
says Milli.

Four stinkbugs are
behind the rocket!

Team Umizoomi puts
the stinkbugs
in the police wagon.

Four stinkbugs are
in the clock shop!
The shop is really stinky!

Bot launches his Robo Net!

# Bot catches
# four stinkbugs.

Four stinkbugs are
in the post office!
One stinkbug is in
an envelope.

Geo searches
with his flashlight.
Three stinkbugs are
hiding in a package.

Team Umizoomi has caught
all twelve stinkbugs.

1, 2, 3, 4, 5, 6,
7, 8, 9, 10, 11, 12!

Team Umizoomi takes
the stinkbugs
to the garbage dump.

The stinkbugs love
the dump!
"It's the stinkiest place
in Umi City," says Bot.

The UmiCops are happy to help!
"I smell a celebration coming on," says Bot.
Everybody Crazy Shake!